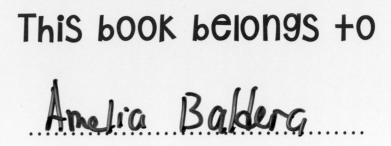

This book belongs to

Amelia Baldera

Written by Rosie Greening.
Illustrated by Stuart Lynch.

We are the grOOvicOrns!

ROSIE GREENING ★ STUART LYNCH

make
believe
ideas

Everyone **loves** unicorns. They always make a fuss. But you know who **should** be famous?

I ♥ unicorns!

but they make
amazing
slides!

Unicorns sign hoofprints,

My Unicorn Scrapbook

To Rabbit,
Love Glitter

Show-off.

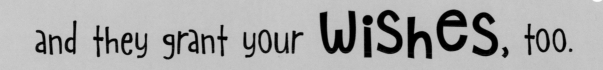

and they grant your **wishes**, too.

HAPPY BIRTHDAY

We don't have
magic powers,

but we still make **dreams** come true!

The unicorns build
palaces

with sweet
marshmallow walls.

No adoring
fans allowed

EEW, unicorn
palaces are
GROSS!

We have **multicolored** tents

All Welcome

The unicorns
bring
sunshine
everywhere
they go.

The sun is
super boring.
You know what's better?

SNOW!

It's **hard** to be a
unicorn —
we have a **lot** to do.

There's **never**
any time to play.
We wish we were
like YOU!

Wow, dancing is fun!

This is how you
disco-dance...

Nice rainbow, Ronald!

and this is how you Sliiiiiiiiide.

EVERYthing
is much more fun
if we PLAY side by side!

Everyone is different, but special in their way.

So let's learn from one another and have more fun every day!